The
Monster
Encyclopedia

written by Dave Branson
illustrated by Tom Bartimole

GREENE BARK PRESS

The Monster Enclopedia

Publisher's Catalog-in-Publication
(Provided by Quality Books Inc.,)

Branson, Dave
    The Monster Enclopedia / Dave Branson; [illustrated by Tom Bartimole]. -- 1st ed.
    p. cm.
    SUMMARY: A compendiaum of newly-imagined monsters, including the Cry-alotis, the Jizzymo,
and the Kissalipis, all of whom exhibit antisocial behaviors. Describes the beasts' habitats, favorite foosd, and
favorite activities.
    Preassigned LCCN: 98-71906
    ISBN: 1-880851-35-0

    I. Monsters--Juvenile fiction. I. Bartimole, Tom.   II.Title.

PZ7.B7377Mo 1998   [E]
                                         QB198.792

To my awesome mother, Mary Branson.
You are my best friend in the world.
This book would not have been possible without you.
I love you, Mom.
–D. B.

To Clarissa.
–T. B.

WELCOME READER!

Inside these pages you will meet the monsters that inhabit our planet. Some will surprise you. Some will make you laugh. Some will make sharing your room with your little sister or brother a good idea.

These strange and sometimes silly monsters have been classified in the following pages to help you, the reader, know which ones to look for and which ones to avoid at all costs.

So prepare to plunge into the realm of the weird, the world of the wonderful, the pages of peril the magical mayhem of monsters. At all times and without exception, follow the monster rules on the next page. Remember, you have been forewarned!

MONSTER RULES TO
FOLLOW AT ALL COSTS

1. Never read this book in the dark.

2. Always have monster food ready to feed those who may want to eat you.

3. Never, never set a monster trap! You never know what you might catch.

4. If you encounter an unfriendly monster, say these magic word—"Zipple Doodle"—to make it go away.

5. The most important rule is to have fun while reading these magical pages, and don't be afraid: monsters are only as real as you make them.

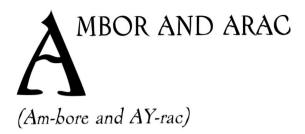

AMBOR AND ARAC

(Am-bore and AY-rac)

DESCRIPTION: These two little titan twins spend most of their time fighting. Rarely does a day pass without Ambor and Arac having a slugfest in the jungle where they live. But neither ever wins a fight. They just fight and fight and fight until they get tired and fall asleep. In the morning, they start fighting again. They fight so much they don't have time to ride bikes or finger-paint or have milk and graham crackers. They just fight.

HELPFUL HINTS: Don't worry about meeting Ambor and Arac because they live in a jungle. And, if you visit the jungle, they'll probably be too busy fighting to notice you. But just in case, keep your distance—or their fight may include you.

HABITAT: Jungles or backyards where brothers and sisters fight.

FAVORITE FOOD: Fruit.

FAVORITE ACTIVITIES: Brawling, boxing, wrestling.

The
BURP-A-LURP

(BURP-uh-LURP)

DESCRIPTION: The Burp-a-Lurp is true to his name. He burps every chance he gets. And when he burps, this monster never says "excuse me" or "I'm sorry." He's famous for his three-cans-of-soda-and-two-pizzas burp. The Burp-a-Lurp loves to burp and blame it on other people.

The rude Burp-a-Lurp has probably gotten you in trouble a few times with his loud, long burps. Since he is invisible, parents sometimes think theses awful burps are coming from their children.

HELPFUL HINTS: The Burp-a-Lurp is trouble with a capital "T". He wants to get you into trouble by burping and blaming it on you. Unless you want to get blamed for the Burp-a Lurp's rude sounds, and miss dessert or TV for a night, cover your mouth when you think this monster is about to make noise.

HABITAT: Crowded restaurants and at the dinner table, especially when grandma visits.

FAVORITE FOODS: Soda, pizza, beans.

FAVORITE ACTIVITIES: Burping, belching, and other gaseous mischief.

The RY-ALOTIS

(KRI-uh-lot-is)

DESCRIPTION: The Cry-alotis is a timid monster who spends time thinking about sad things, like the broccoli and spinach he has to eat. He cries because he will have to eat you if you cross his path. He always has a runny nose and tears on his face.

HELPFUL HINTS: If you encounter the Cry-alotis, tell him a sad story, like how much homework you did last night. While he's sobbing, you can get away.

HABITAT: Weeping willow trees.

FAVORITE FOOD: Salty pretzels.

FAVORITE ACTIVITIES: Sighing, crying, sobbing.

The DUTZ

(Durst)

DESCRIPTION: The Dutz is the clumsiest of all monsters. It bumps into everything. If you hear a noise in your house in the middle of the night, and in the morning a table or chair is overturned, you know a Dutz has visited you.

The Dutz is so clumsy because its feet are twice as big as the rest of its body. It can't walk without falling down.

HELPFUL HINTS: Feel sorry for the poor Dutz. Do everything you can to help it walk upright. Put your toys away before you go to bed. Don't leave your shoes in the middle of the floor. Put banana peels in the trash. The Dutz will thank you by staying quiet all night.

HABITAT: Unfortunately, messy places.

FAVORITE FOODS: Anything she trips over.

FAVORITE ACTIVITIES: Tumbling, falling, slipping

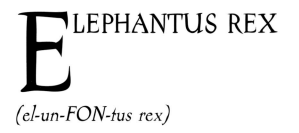LEPHANTUS REX

(el-un-FON-tus rex)

DESCRIPTION: This massive monster lived many years ago. He was ten times bigger than any dinosaur, and he had a polka dot trunk like an elephant. Elephantus Rex caused only trouble in the time he roamed the earth. He was so big he stepped on everything he walked by. Every evening, before bedtime, he picked trees from between his toes. And every morning, he scraped dinosaurs off his tail where he had rolled over on them during the night.

The Elephantus Rex died out when, one night, he rolled over in bed and squashed himself.

HELPFUL HINTS: You have no reason to be wary of this monster because he's been gone for years. Just be glad he is.

HABITAT: Forests.

FAVORITE FOOD: None.

FAVORITE ACTIVITY: None.

FRY-A-FLY

(FRI-uh-fli)

DESCRIPTION: Everybody loves the Fry-a-Fly. He's a hungry monster who's constantly searching for annoying flies. If a fly lands on the cookies your mother is baking, "Slurp!", the Fry-a-Fly is there. Another fly lights on your grandpa's nose. "Swoop!" A Fry-a Fly rescues him.

The Fry-a-Fly loves fried flies, baked flies, boiled flies, steamed flies, fricasseed flies, and flies under glass. He likes them on whole wheat and sesame seed buns. He enjoys fly-and-peanut butter sandwiches and—his personal favorite—French flies.

HELPFUL HINTS: Although a Fry-a-Fly makes life more comfortable, he needs to learn to eat his vegetables. If your house is fly-free, the Fry-a-Fly will get hungry enough for cauliflower and green beans. So close the door behind you when you come in your house.

HABITAT: Where flies abound.

FAVORITE FOOD: Flies

FAVORITE ACTIVITY: Fly fishing.

The LOWING GLOON

(GLOOHN)

DESCRIPTION: If you're outside at night and see something glowing, there may be a Gloon nearby. The Gloon looks like the moon, but glows even brighter. The tiny Gloon is round like the moon. She has no arms or legs, so she has to roll.

This little monster is afraid of you. The Gloon is often mistaken for a cookie. Many Gloons have met their doom at the hands of hungry children.

HELPFUL HINTS: When you're hungry for a sugar, raisin oatmeal, or chocolate chip cookie, please make sure it's a cookie your eating and not a Gloon.

HABITAT: Kitchens, especially cookie jars.

FAVORITE FOODS: Cookies and milk.

FAVORITE ACTIVITIES: Rolling and glowing.

Heebie Geebie

(HEE-bee JEE-bee)

DESCRIPTION: At first glance, this monster is scary. The Heebie Geebie is big and ugly and mean. He's a horrible shade of green.

The Heebie Geebie likes to hide under a bed or in the closet. He waits until you are not expecting company, then he jumps out and yells "BOOOOOOOO!" This big bully wants you to run so he can chase you.

HELPFUL HINTS: There's something about the Heebie Geebie that he hopes you don't find out: He's really scared of you. If you show him you're not afraid, he'll run from you. The magic words "Zipple Doodle" work well with this monster.

HABITAT: Closets and under beds.

FAVORITE FOOD: The dust under your bed.

FAVORITE ACTIVITY: Pretending to be scary.

I Mr. IDIN

(EYE-din)

DESCRIPTION: Make way for Idin, king of the monsters! Idin is the big cheese of the monster world. All monsters listen to what he says. You may even call him the principal of monsters, but be sure you call him mister or sir.

Mr. Idin has a lot of responsibilities telling other monsters what to do. His gigantic army of creatures assures that MR. Idin is always safe, even though he could conquer any monster any day.

HELPFUL HINTS: If you see Sir Idin, bow to the king. Give him your lunch. Make him happy See that he smiles. Of course, if you feel mean, you can always say "Zipple Doodle" and make him disappear.

HABITAT: The monster palace in Eerie, Pennsylvania.

FAVORITE FOODS: Any meal fit for a king.

FAVORITE ACTIVITY: Ruling the monster world.

IZZYMO

(JIZ-ee-mo)

DESCRIPTION: The Jizzymo is a thief, plain and simple. He will steal anything. His collection of other people's thing is the size of a large mountain in Colorado. He has cats' hats, bears' beanbags, and your sister's dolls. He has lots of tiny screws and nails that your father has been looking for. He has the baseball cards you wanted to save.

If this little bandit sees something he wants, he opens up a window, sneaks inside, and just takes it! If your favorite tyrannosaurus rex toy is missing, a Jizzymo may just have it.

HELPFUL HINTS: If a Jizzymo steals from you, there are two things you could do. You could follow him back to his cave and recapture your treasure. (Be sure that's all you take or you could become a Jizzymo yourself!) Or you could repeat the Jizzymo's Vanishing formula: "Teeny, tiny Jizzymo. Now I have you by the toe. You tried to steal my toys today. But I won't tell if you go away."

HABITAT: Caves or, when caves are scarce, underground.

FAVORITE FOOD: Children's lunch.

FAVORITE ACTIVITIES: Sneaking, stealing, borrowing, taking.

Kissalipis

(KISS-uh-lip-us)

DESCRIPTION: All children should watch out for the Kissalipis, also known as the love monster. The Kissalipis likes to make little boys and girls kiss each other! Yuk! If a girl or boy kisses you on the playground you'll know that a Kissalipis is to blame.

HELPFUL HINTS: If you don't want to kiss someone or have someone kiss you, stay away from the Kissalipis. You won't be able to fight him forever but for now, when you see someone coming toward you with lips puckered; run or you will get a big smooch—a gift from the Kissalipis.

HABITAT: Playgrounds.

FAVORITE FOOD: Chocolate kisses.

FAVORITE ACTIVITIES: Kissy games.

The L UMP

(LUMP)

DESCRIPTION: All monsters should do something, right? They should, but they don't. The Lump is good only at doing nothing.

But she does nothing well. The Lump looks like a tree stump, a great shape for her because she never moves. Once, thirteen years ago, she moved. But the Lump decided moving was too much trouble, so now she stays in one position all the time.

She's not ugly or dangerous or even funny. She's just there.

HELPFUL HINTS: Why worry about the Lump? She can't hurt you or steal your toys or make you burp. If you see a tree stump in the backyard, it may be a Lump. But do you really care?

HABITAT: Wooded areas.

FAVORITE FOOD: Only air, since she won't move to get anything else.

FAVORITE ACTIVITY: Nothing.

MYROMORPH

(MY-row-morf)

DESCRIPTION: The coolest of all monsters is the Myromorph. This guy can be big or small. He can change into anything he likes—a dog, a lamp, a rocket ship, or even a kid like you. The Myromorph can go anywhere he wants to without being recognized. He can be something naughty, then change into something else, and no one can find him. All monsters wish they were Myromorphs.

HELPFUL HINTS: Don't try to look for the Myromorph. You'll never know what he looks like or what he'll be next. Wouldn't it be fun to be a Myromorph?

HABITAT: Anywhere and everywhere.

FAVORITE FOOD: Chameleons.

FAVORITE ACTIVITY: His activities are always changing.

Nosmeller

(noz-SMEL-ur)

DESCRIPTION: This funny monster, Nosmeller, doesn't have a nose, so he can be around anything stinky and not mind— a skunk, or even your little brother!

Nosmeller eats anything he wants because he can't smell it. So watch out that could include you.

HELPFUL HINTS: Nosmeller is always looking for a nose so he can smell. He isn't picky about noses. He would take a long nose or a short one. He'd be happy with a round nose, and elephant's nose, or even your nose. He notices noses when you blow them or sneeze. So be sure to cover your nose with a tissue to protect it from the Nosmeller.

HABITAT: Smelly places.

FAVORITE FOOD: Anything.

FAVORITE ACTIVITY: Nose-napping.

# OLLIEOLIVE

(Ah-lee-AHL-iv)

DESCRIPTION: The Ollieolive is the sweetest, kindest, gentlest monster you will find anywhere. She would rather bake cookies than eat people. Her teeth are tiny and soft—she could eat your pizza if she wanted to (which, of course, she's too polite to do). When she's not cooking, she spends her time cleaning house and watering flowers.

Ollieolive is known throughout the monster kingdom for her creative cookies, baked frog, and roach surprise.

HELPFUL HINTS: Maybe someday you'll run into Ollieolive. She will treat you to a nice meal, maybe rat tail stew and snake pie. If you are especially polite and say "thank you," you may even get some of her famous lizard cookies and a hot mouse sundae for dessert. Enjoy your meal.

HABITAT: In a nice, clean house.

FAVORITE FOODS: Anything she cooks.

FAVORITE ACTIVITIES: Cooking, cleaning, gardening.

The PICKETT

(PIK-it)

DESCRIPTION: The Pickett keeps busy pulling surprises out of her nose. With extra long fingers she doesn't leave anything in there.

Picketts have a bad habit of leaving nose treasures under desks and chairs. They love to watch people's faces when they find them.

HELPFUL HINTS: The Pickett is one wacky monster. No one wants to find one of her gifts, so don't look under your desk at school. You just may find one.

If a Pickett passes by, toss her a tissue. Then make a fast getaway.

HABITAT: Classrooms.

FAVORITE FOODS: Tissues and handkerchiefs.

FAVORITE ACTIVITY: Hiding her treasures.

QUIRMO

(QUERE-more)

DESCRIPTION: Quirmo knows everything that's going on. He knows who likes who, what you had for breakfast, and who got in trouble at school. He knows your mother's age and he'll tell it, too! He even knows how much your grandmother weighs.

Quirmo listens to everything people say. If you tell someone a secret and a Quirmo is nearby, he'll find out your secret, and he'll tell too.

HELPFUL HINTS: If you know a secret, do not tell it. A busybody Quirmo may be nearby.

HABITAT: Anywhere people are.

FAVORITE FOOD: Secret Sauce.

FAVORITE ACTIVITIES: Spying, eavesdropping, telling secrets.

RAY COOL, JR.

(RAY KOOL)

DESCRIPTION: Ray Cool, Jr., is one party animal. He's the most popular of all monsters. Cool has fun wherever he goes, but he never finishes his homework. He simply doesn't have time. Even when Cool is sleeping, he dreams of having fun.

The other monsters love to hang around Cool. When Cool starts one of his awesome monster raps, even King Idin starts to boogie down. Cool knows how to have a good time.

Cool is never lonely, until it's time to do homework. Then he can't seem to locate his friends.

HELPFUL HINTS: Ray Cool, Jr., isn't hard to find. Where there's a party of any kind of fun, you'll find Cool. Just toss him a pair of sunglasses, and he'll turn into a party animal. Maybe he'll sing one of his famous monster raps for you.

HABITAT: Wherever there's fun.

FAVORITE FOODS: Cool things like frozen yogurt and peppermints.

FAVORITE ACTIVITY: Being the party guy.

STINKY BLINKY

(STEEN-kee BLEEN-kee)

DESCRIPTION: Stinky Blinky lives by himself. The reason? He smells like your father's sweat socks when they've been in the laundry hamper for a week.

Stinky has no friends, except Nosmeller. He likes to play tricks on children like you. He'll sprinkle his magic stink dust around your bedroom, even in your shoes, just for his enjoyment.

HELPFUL HINTS: Avoid Stinky when at all possible. He isn't hard to spot: when your nose starts to wrinkle, and your eyes start to swim, Stinky is nearby. If you encounter Stinky, remember to shout "Zipple Doodle" and pinch your nose shut until he goes away.

HABITAT: Gym lockers and city dumps.

FAVORITE FOODS: Old shoes and skunks.

FAVORITE ACTIVITY: Making nice kids' rooms smell stinky.

TEACHER'S PET

(TEE-churz PET)

DESCRIPTION: The teacher's Pet gives your teacher all the ideas he or she needs to think of homework and other assignments. The Teacher's Pet is friendly, but she loves to watch you work.

HELPFUL HINTS: You will encounter the Teacher's Pet. There is no way to avoid her. Remember that your favorite teacher loves her, so maybe she's not too bad. If you let her sit next to you, she'll help you do better in school. And if you are foolish enough to tell her to go away, your teacher might ask another monster for ideas—or make you do the same homework over and over and over and over and over.

HABITAT: A teacher's desk.

FAVORITE FOOD: Apples.

FAVORITE ACTIVITY: Homework.

UNDY LUNDY

(UN-dee LUN-dee)

DESCRIPTION: This quiet monster has one important job in life: He lives in your dresser and guards your underwear from thieves like the Jizzymo. You can thank the Undy Laundy that your underwear doesn't disappear more often than it does.

As useful as he is, the Undy Lundy has a weakness. He eats socks. For example, if your dad washes clothes and can find only one of his brown socks, you can bet the Undy Lundy is sitting on top of the dryer, full and satisfied.

HELPFUL HINTS: Losing socks is no fun. While it's good that the Undy Lundy guards underwear, you may want to toss an old sock or two in with your underwear to keep Undy Lundy well-fed.

HABITAT: Dryers and drawer, where underwear is kept.

FAVORITE FOOD: Socks.

FAVORITE ACTIVITY: Guarding underwear.

Verius Uglius

(VAIR-ee-us UG-lee-us)

DESCRIPTION: Compared to Verius Uglius, a pet rock is beautiful. People can't agree on exactly what makes him so ugly. Maybe the five eyes scattered around his head or his eight yellow horns. Or the pink and blue hair on his head—and in his ears and nose. Whatever it is, this is one ugly guy.

But the funny thing about Uglius is that he thinks he looks great. In fact, he spends most of his days looking at himself in the shiny toaster.

HELPFUL HINTS: If you see the Verius Uglius, don't mention his looks or you may regret it. His teeth are sharp, and he's not afraid to bite. The best way to get past him is to tell him how handsome he looks. If you don't want to tell a lie, cross your fingers as you pass.

HABITAT: Near toasters and other shiny objects.

FAVORITE FOOD: Anything that laughs at him.

FAVORITE ACTIVITY: Admiring himself.

The W AHSNER

(wAH-snr)

DESCRIPTION: No one knows whether to call this creature a monster or a helicopter. The Wahsner flies using the propeller sticking out of his head and creates quite a stir when soaring through the air with the crows and eagles.

The Wahsner enjoys snacking on birds. He chomps them out of the air as he flies by. The Wahsner is so big that he sometimes eats an airplane by mistake.

HELPFUL HINTS: When the Wahsner is finished eating, he drops his leftovers on the ground. So watch out when you're outdoors. You may have to dodge a piece of blackbird, oriole, or even airplane parts.

HABITAT: The sky.

FAVORITE FOODS: All types of birds and airplanes, especially 747s.

FAVORITE ACTIVITIES: Flying and eating.

XYLERPHU

(ZY-lur-foo)

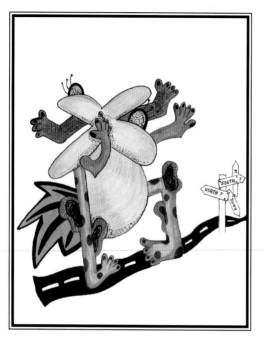

DESCRIPTION: The Xylerphu is as mixed up as her name. Her feet are where her ears should be. She has a hand for a nose and her eyes are on the back of her head. Her ears are on her knees, and her bellybutton is between her eyes.

When you see the Xylerphu, you can't tell whether she's coming or going. This weird monster loves to eat books, so guard this book carefully.

HELPFUL HINTS: If a Xylerphu comes after you, show her a mirror. The Xylerphu will think she's going the wrong direction and turn around and run in the opposite direction.

HABITAT: Open spaces where she can turn around quickly.

FAVORITE FOODS: Pineapple upside down cake, books.

FAVORITE ACTIVITY: Trying to find the right direction.

YAK-A-YAK

(YAK-uh-YAK)

DESCRIPTION: This creature is the noisiest of all monsters. She talks and talks without giving anyone else a chance. The Yak-a-Yak is skinny because she seldom stops talking long enough to eat. She will talk to anyone or anything, even to chairs, cars, and bookcases.

HELPFUL HINTS: The Yak-a-Yak is just boring. The only good time to talk to her is when you are ready to fall asleep.

HABITAT: Telephones.

FAVORITE FOOD: None.

FAVORITE ACTIVITIES: Talking, talking, and talking.

Z YX

(ZIX)

DESCRIPTION: The Zyx is the hardest of all monsters to find. Like the Burp-a-Lurp, he's invisible. But unlike the Burp-a-Lurp, he doesn't wear shoes. The part of him you can see is his whiskers, which look like a grandfather's thick, white mustache.

Zyx likes to play pranks on kids like you. He may come up behind you and give you a poke or a pinch, which you can blame on your little brother. Never underestimate the Zyx. There's no end to the things he can do and not be caught.

HELPFUL HINTS: If someone changes the answers on your homework or you see your dog wearing a dress, there may be a Zyx living nearby.

There's only one way to get rid of a Zyx. Wait till you suspect he's outside (If you do this inside, you may wish you were a Zyx, too.). Then throw maple syrup on him. As he starts eating it, he will begin to turn brown like the syrup. (Blueberry syrup will also work, although he will turn blue.) Then eat him quickly. He makes a delicious pancake.

HABITAT: He could be anywhere.

FAVORITE FOOD: Anything but pancakes.

FAVORITE ACTIVITY: Bothering you.

YOU MADE IT!
YOU REACHED THE END!

You have just completed a thorough study of monsters and now you'll know how to deal with them. If you meet what appears to be a monster and he or she is not listed here from A to Z in this book, it should be viewed with suspicion.

Most of all, remember that any monster will disappear if you say the magic words "Zipple Doodle."